TOP SECRET GRAPHICA MYSTERIES

CASEBOOK: ATLANTIS

Script by Justine and Ron Fontes

Layouts and Designs by Ron Fontes

Skyview Books

an imprint of
WINDMILL BOOKS
New York

Published in 2010 by Windmill Books, LLC
303 Park Avenue South, Suite # 1280
New York, NY 10010-3657

CREDITS:
Script by Justine and Ron Fontes
Layouts and designs by Ron Fontes
Art by Planman, Ltd.

Publisher Cataloging in Publication

Fontes, Justine
        Casebook—Atlantis. – School and library ed. / script by Justine and Ron Fontes
; layouts and designs by Ron Fontes.
p.   cm. – (Top secret graphica mysteries)
Summary: Einstein and his friends from the Windmill Bakery use their virtual
visors to investigate Atlantis, a legendary island said to have been built by the god Poseidon.
ISBN 978-1-60754-588-0. – ISBN 978-1-60754-590-3 (pbk.)
ISBN 978-1-60754-589-7 (6-pack)
        1.   Atlantis (Legendary place)—Juvenile fiction   2. Graphic novels
[1. Atlantis (Legendary place)—Fiction   2. Graphic novels]   I. Fontes, Ron
II. Title   III. Title: Atlantis   IV. Series
        741.5/973—dc22

Manufactured in the United States of America

CPSIA Compliance Information: Batch #BW10W: For further information contact Windmill Books, New York, New York at 1-866-478-0556.

MAY 1 9 2010

CONTENTS

Welcome to the Windmill Bakery

Edward Icarus Stein is known as "Einstein" because of his initials "E.I." and his last name, and because he loves science the way fanatical fans love sports. Einstein dedicates his waking hours to observing as much as he can of all the strange things just beyond human knowledge, because "that's the discovery zone," as he calls it. Einstein aspires to nothing less than living up to his nickname and coming up with a truly groundbreaking scientific discovery. So far this brilliant seventh grader's best invention is the Virtual Visors he and his friends use to explore strange phenomena. Einstein's parents own the local bakery where the friends meet.

The Windmill Bakery is a cozy place where friends and neighbors buy homemade goodies to go or to eat on the premises. Einstein's kindhearted parents make everyone feel welcome, especially the friends who understand their exceptional son and share his appetite for discovery!

"Spacey Tracy" Lee saw a UFO when she was seven. Her parents tried to dismiss the incident as a "waking dream." But Tracy knew what she saw and it inspired her to investigate the UFO phenomenon. The more she learned, the more fascinated she became. She earned her nickname by constantly talking about UFOs. Tracy hopes to become a reporter when she grows up so she can continue to explore the unknown. A straight-A student, Tracy enjoys swimming, gymnastics, and playing the cello. Now that she's "more mature" and hoping to lose the silly nickname, Tracy shares the experience that changed her life forever only with her Virtual Visor buddies.

Clarita Gonzales knows that Indiana Jones and Lara Croft aren't real people, but that doesn't stop this seventh grader from wanting to be an adventurous archaeologist. Clarita's parents will support any path she chooses, as long as she gets a good education. Unfortunately, school isn't her strong point. During most classes, Clarita's mind wanders to, as she puts it, "more exciting places—like Atlantis!" A tomboy thanks to her three older brothers and one younger brother, Clarita is a great soccer player and is also into martial arts. Her interest in archaeology extends to architecture, artifacts, cooking, and all forms of culture. (Clarita would have a crush on Einstein if he wasn't "such a bookworm")!

"Freaky Frank" Phillips earned his nickname because of his uncanny ability to use his "extra senses," a "gift" he inherited from his grandma. Though this eighth grader can't predict the winners of the next SUPERBOWL (or, he admits, "anything really useful"), Frank "knows" when someone is lying or otherwise up to no good. He gets "warnings" before trouble strikes. And sometimes he "sees things that aren't there"—at least to those less sensitive to things like auras and ghosts. Frank isn't sure what he wants to be when he grows up. He enjoys keeping tropical fish and does well in every subject, except math. "Numbers make my head hurt," Frank confesses. Frank spends lots of time with his family and his fish, but he's always up for an adventure with his friends.

The Virtual Visors allow Einstein, Frank, Clarita, and Tracy to pursue their taste for adventure well beyond the boundaries of the bakery. Thanks to Einstein's brilliant software, the visors can simulate all kinds of locations and experiences based on the uploaded facts. Once inside the program, the visors become invisible. When danger gets too intense, the kids can always touch their Virtual Visors to return to the bakery. Sometimes the kids explore in the real world without the visors. But more often they use these devices to explore the mysteries and phenomena that intrigue each member of the group. The Virtual Visors are the ultimate virtual reality research tool, even though you never know what quirky things might happen thanks to Einstein's "Random Adventure Program."

ACCORDING TO LEGEND, PARADISE ONCE EXISTED ON EARTH.

POSEIDON, THE ANCIENT GREEK GOD OF THE SEA AND EARTHQUAKES, RULED THIS BEAUTIFUL ISLAND CONTINENT.

THERE HE MET A MORTAL MAIDEN, CLEITO, WHO LIVED ON A HILL.

I KNOW CLEITO'S ONLY A MORTAL, BUT I'M IN LOVE!

POSEIDON'S SO DIVINE!

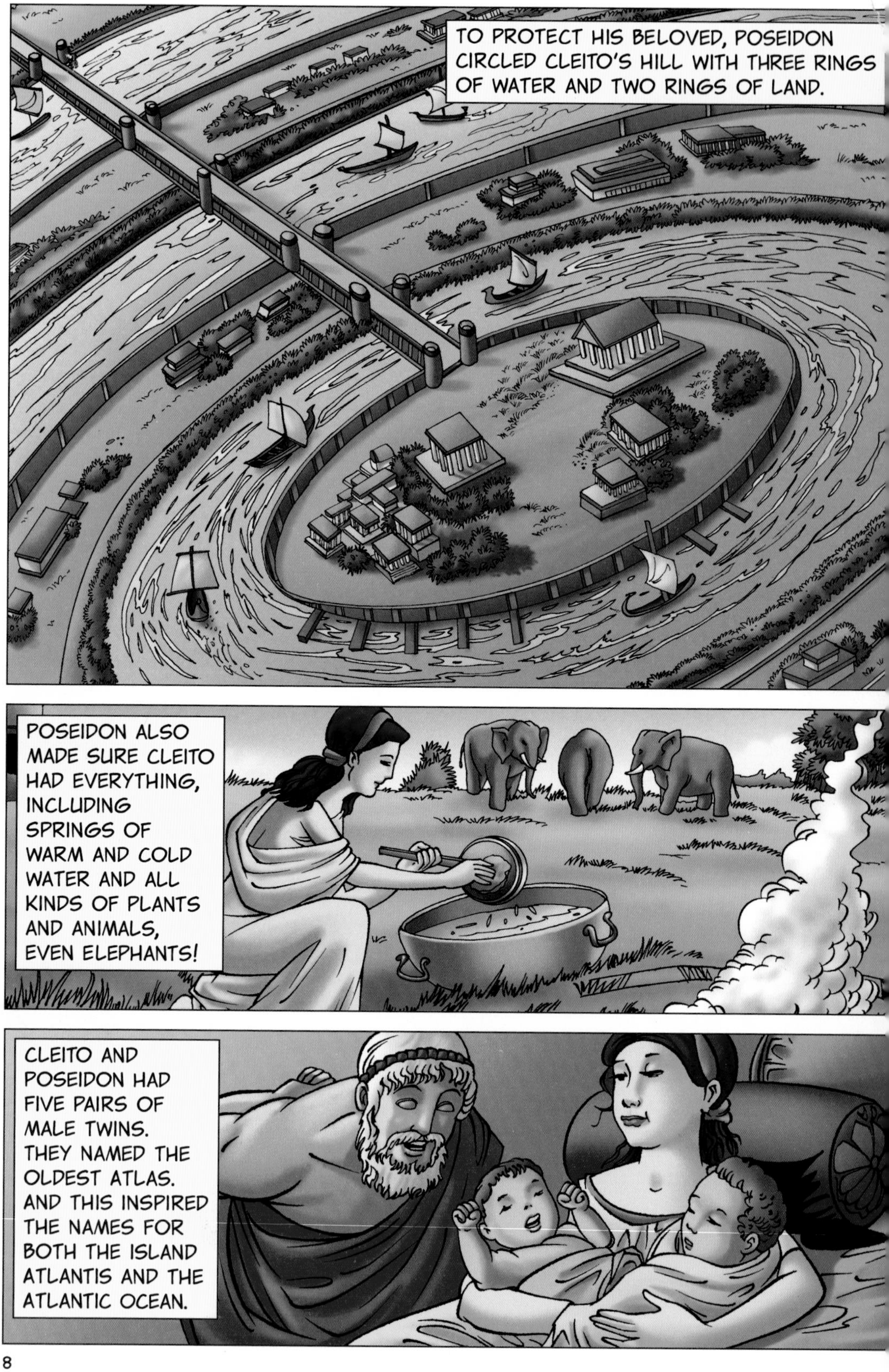

TO PROTECT HIS BELOVED, POSEIDON CIRCLED CLEITO'S HILL WITH THREE RINGS OF WATER AND TWO RINGS OF LAND.

POSEIDON ALSO MADE SURE CLEITO HAD EVERYTHING, INCLUDING SPRINGS OF WARM AND COLD WATER AND ALL KINDS OF PLANTS AND ANIMALS, EVEN ELEPHANTS!

CLEITO AND POSEIDON HAD FIVE PAIRS OF MALE TWINS. THEY NAMED THE OLDEST ATLAS. AND THIS INSPIRED THE NAMES FOR BOTH THE ISLAND ATLANTIS AND THE ATLANTIC OCEAN.

POSEIDON DIVIDED ATLANTIS INTO TEN KINGDOMS, TO BE RULED BY HIS TEN SONS. THESE WISE, GOOD KINGS BUILT BRIDGES, TUNNELS, A HUGE CANAL LINKING THE HARBOR TO THE SEA, AND A GREAT TEMPLE TO POSEIDON.

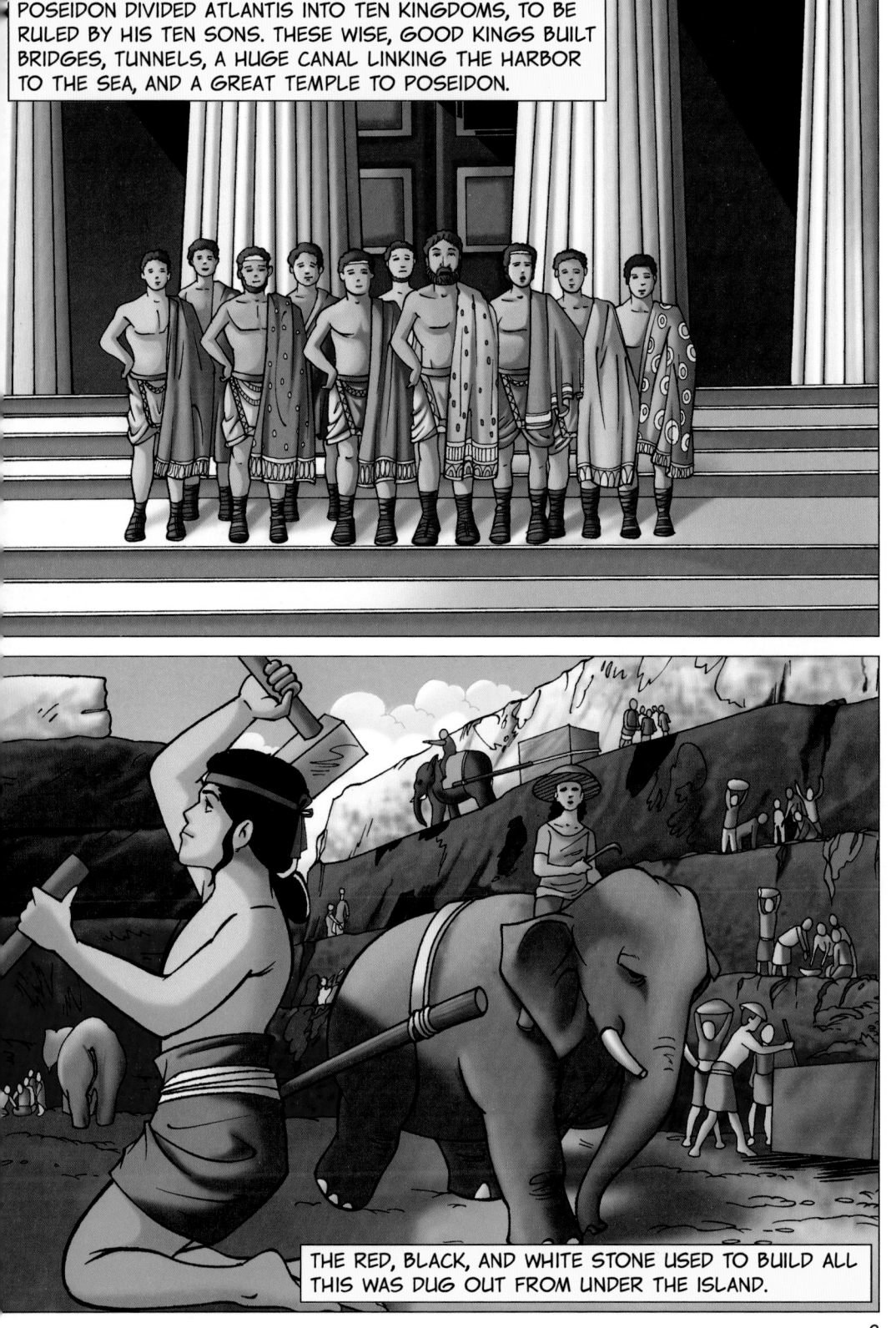

THE RED, BLACK, AND WHITE STONE USED TO BUILD ALL THIS WAS DUG OUT FROM UNDER THE ISLAND.

EVERY FIVE OR SIX YEARS, THE TEN KINGS OF ATLANTIS PERFORMED A STRANGE RITUAL.

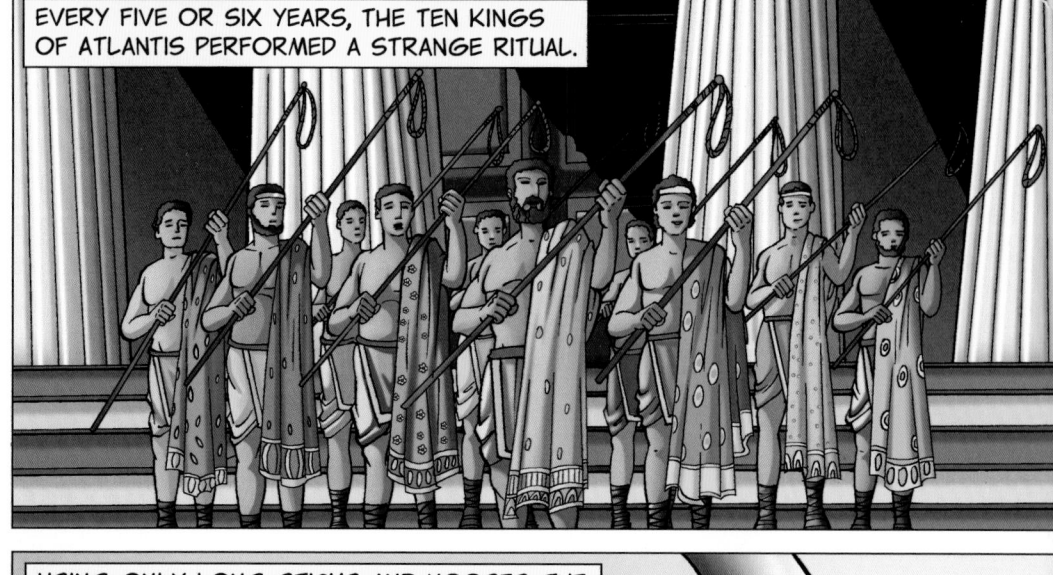

USING ONLY LONG STICKS AND NOOSES, THE KINGS HUNTED BULLS IN POSEIDON'S TEMPLE.

BULLS WERE SACRED TO POSEIDON AND ALSO TO THE ATLANTEANS.

AFTER MANY GENERATIONS THESE ONCE PIOUS PEOPLE BECAME GREEDY AND PROUD. THE ATLANTEANS BUILT UP THEIR ARMY AND. . .

MIGHT MAKES RIGHT—OR AT LEAST RICH!

. . .INVADED THEIR NEIGHBORS!

THIS OFFENDED **ZEUS**, KING OF THE GODS. SO HE GATHERED ALL THE OTHER **OLYMPIANS** AND. . .

HERE'S HOW WE'LL PUNISH THESE PROUD ATLANTEANS. . .

SOON AFTER THAT, THE ATLANTEANS WERE WIPED OUT BY A HUGE DISASTER!

BECAUSE THESE ANCIENT ATHENIANS HAD NO WRITTEN LANGUAGE. . .

. . .YOUR PROUD HISTORY SLIPPED INTO LEGEND.

YOU SHOULD REALLY TRY WRITING ON ROCKS. IT LASTS!

NOW I FEEL EVEN MORE PROUD TO BE FROM ATHENS!

I'LL TELL THIS STORY TO MY FRIENDS AND SOMEONE WILL WRITE IT DOWN.

BUT, AS YOU KNOW, NO ONE DID THIS UNTIL MANY YEARS LATER.

AND HE DIDN'T FINISH IT!

THIS IS ALL JUST STORIES.

WHEN DO WE GET TO THE FACTS?

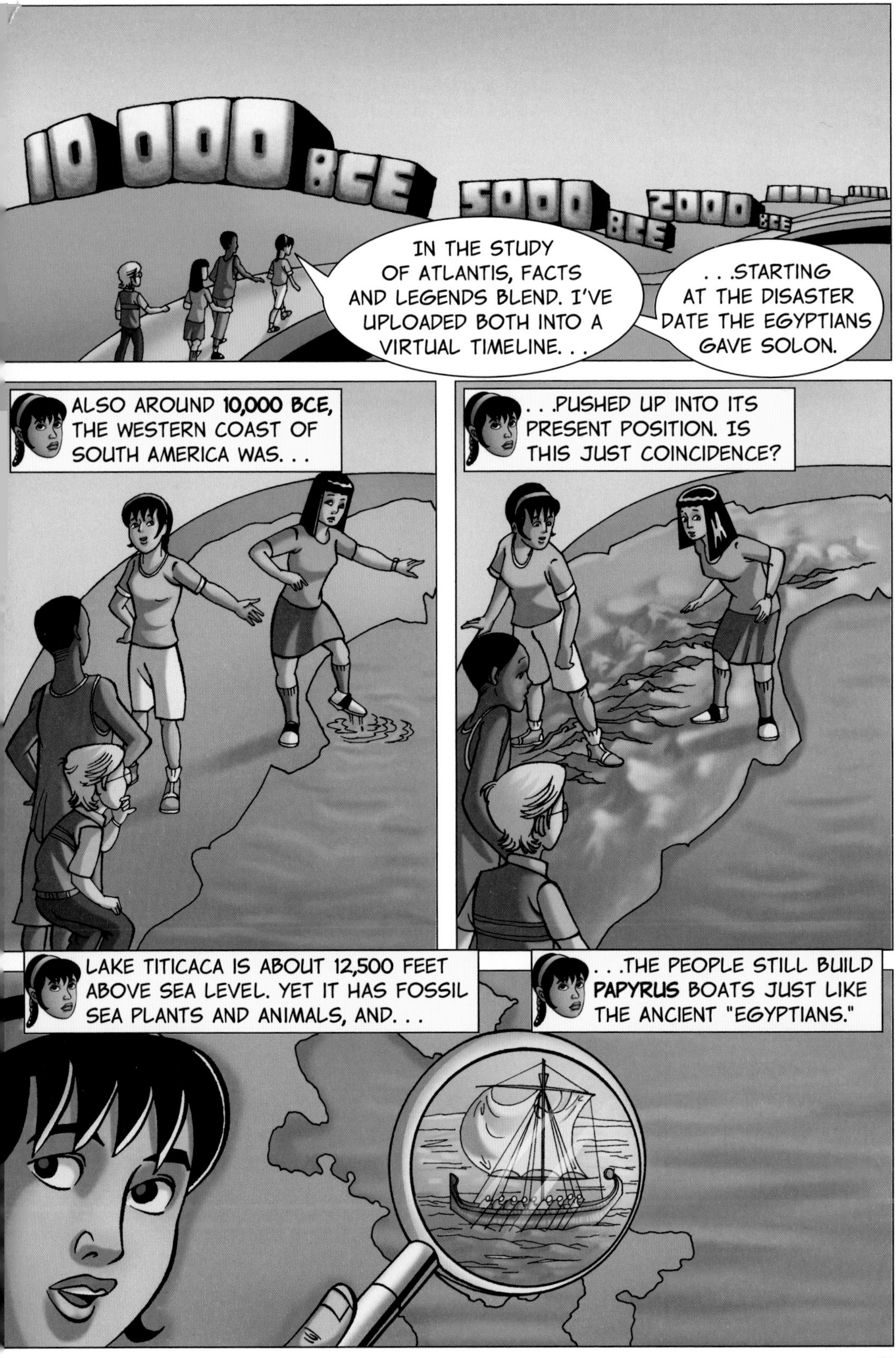

10,000 BCE   5000 BCE   2000 BCE

IN THE STUDY OF ATLANTIS, FACTS AND LEGENDS BLEND. I'VE UPLOADED BOTH INTO A VIRTUAL TIMELINE. . .

. . .STARTING AT THE DISASTER DATE THE EGYPTIANS GAVE SOLON.

ALSO AROUND **10,000 BCE**, THE WESTERN COAST OF SOUTH AMERICA WAS. . .

. . .PUSHED UP INTO ITS PRESENT POSITION. IS THIS JUST COINCIDENCE?

LAKE TITICACA IS ABOUT 12,500 FEET ABOVE SEA LEVEL. YET IT HAS FOSSIL SEA PLANTS AND ANIMALS, AND. . .

. . .THE PEOPLE STILL BUILD **PAPYRUS** BOATS JUST LIKE THE ANCIENT "EGYPTIANS."

COULD THESE HAVE BEEN CARRIED UP FROM ATLANTIS BY A TIDAL WAVE BIG ENOUGH TO SINK A CONTINENT?
LET'S KEEP MOVING YOU'RE GOING TO LOVE **2500 BCE**!
WHAT'S SO GREAT ABOUT THEN?
2500 BCE

THE **MINOANS**! THIS IS WHAT THEIR **PALACE AT KNOSSOS** MIGHT HAVE LOOKED LIKE.
IT'S SO BEAUTIFUL!
IT'S MORE LIKE A WHOLE CITY THAN A PALACE.
WERE THE MINOANS REALLY SO ADVANCED?

THE MINOANS DIDN'T JUST HAVE PRETTY WALL PAINTINGS. . .

. . .THEY HAD HOT AND COLD RUNNING WATER!
MINOAN BUILDINGS WERE DESIGNED FOR LIGHT AND NATURAL AIR CONDITIONING.

21

NO! THE OLMECS WERE EVEN MORE MYSTERIOUS THAN THE MAYANS, WHO BUILT AN EMPIRE OF...

...AMAZING CITIES THAT THRIVED FOR ABOUT 1,400 YEARS UNTIL...

...FOR SOME REASON, THE MAYANS DISAPPEARED!

THERE ARE MANY THEORIES.

THE MAYANS AND OLMECS WEREN'T THE ONLY MYSTERIOUS, ADVANCED CULTURES IN SOUTH AMERICA.

IN THE 1200S, THE **INCAS** FOUND...

HE S YOU HERE, ARITA!

HOLD ON, WHO ARE THE INCAS?

LOOK WHO'S USING CONFUSING TERMS NOW!

THE INCAS WERE THE NATIVES OF PERU, WHO LIVED THERE BEFORE THE SPANISH *CONQUISTADORES* ARRIVED.

AND THAT'S AN EVEN BIGGER WORD!

IT JUST MEANS "CONQUERORS." BUT WE'RE NOT READY FOR THE 1500S YET.

NEAR BOLIVIA, AT **TIAHUANACO**, THE INCAS FOUND SOME AWESOME RUINS!

WHO BUILT THESE HUGE THINGS?

WHY?

HOW?

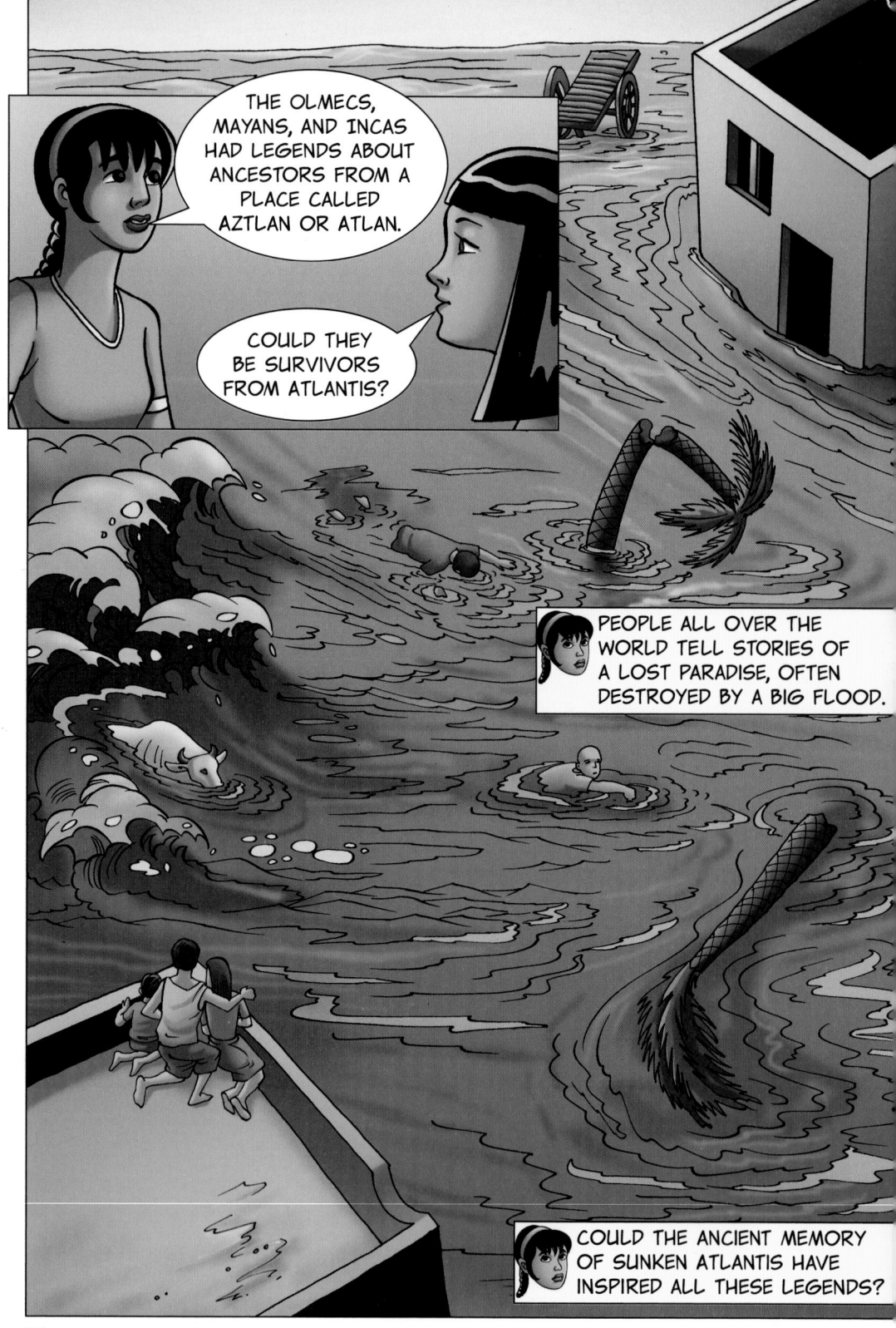

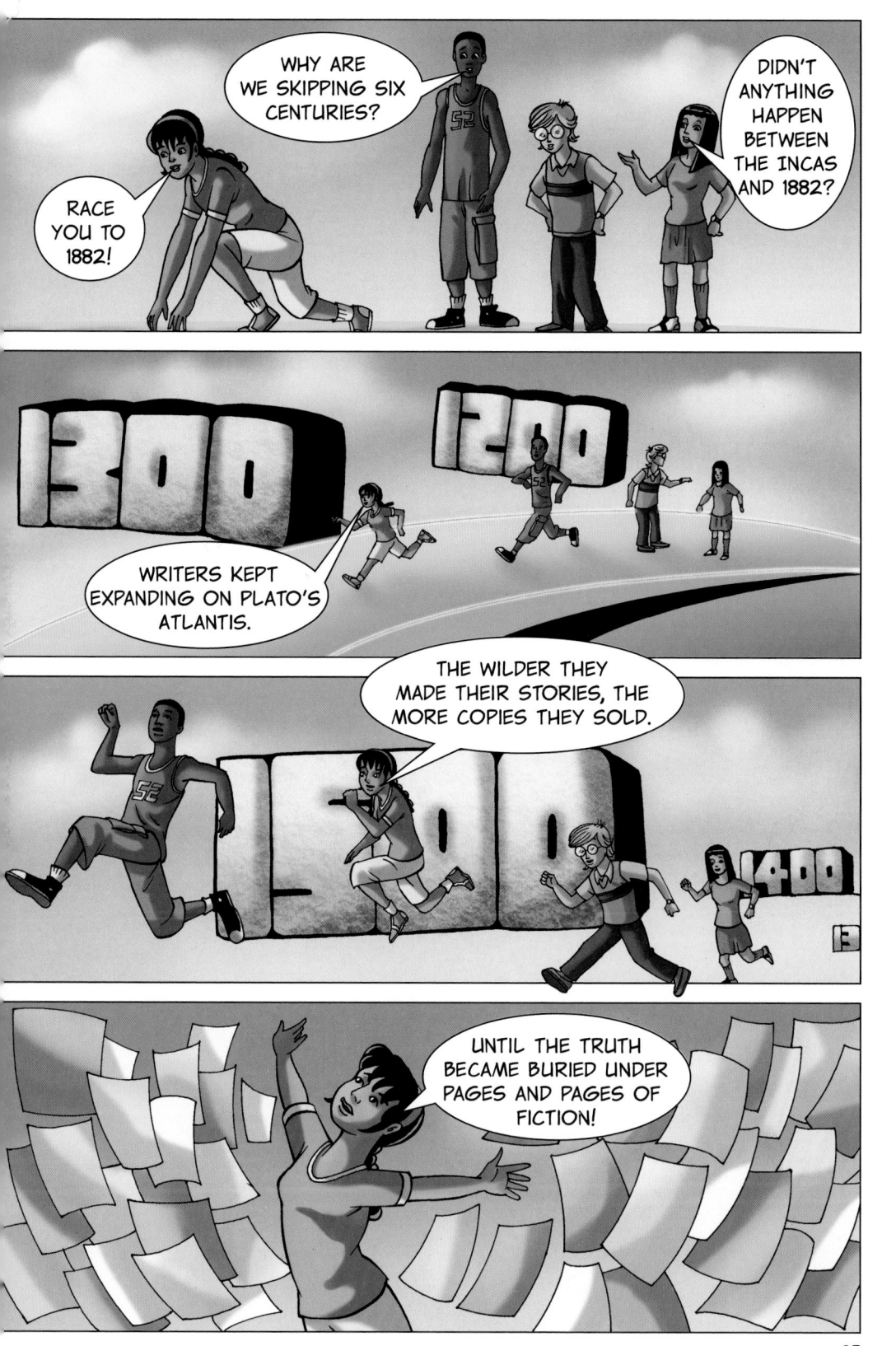

WHAT HAPPENED IN 1882?

IT'S MORE OF A WHO THAN A WHAT. IGNATIUS DONNELLY WAS

A CURIOUS U.S. CONGRESSMAN WHO. . .

. . .READ ALL ABOUT ATLANTIS: ITS ARCHAEOLOGY, OCEANOGRAPHY, GEOLOGY, HISTORY, MYTHOLOGY, ZOOLOGY, BOTANY, AND MORE.

THEN DONNELLY PUT EVERYTHING HE LEARNED TOGETHER IN ONE BOOK THAT BECAME AN INTERNATIONAL BEST-SELLER.

ATLANTIS
THE ANTEDILUVIAN WORLD

IGNATIUS DONNELLY

BUT HAVEN'T SOME OF DONNELLY'S "FACTS" BEEN PROVEN WRONG?

YES, BUT HIS BOOK STILL INSPIRES PEOPLE TO LEARN ABOUT ATLANTIS!

THE FOUR BIG BLASTS THAT ENDED THE ERUPTION SHOOK DOORS AND WINDOWS 100 MILES AWAY. THEY ARE THE LOUDEST NOISES EVER RECORDED ON EARTH.

THE **TSUNAMI** CAUSED BY KRAKATOA KILLED 36,380 PEOPLE AND SWEPT AWAY 300 TOWNS AND VILLAGES!

DUST FELL FROM THE SKY FOR A DOZEN DAYS AFTER THE LAST BLAST. ALL OVER THE WORLD, PEOPLE MARVELED AT SPECTACULAR GREEN SUNRISES!

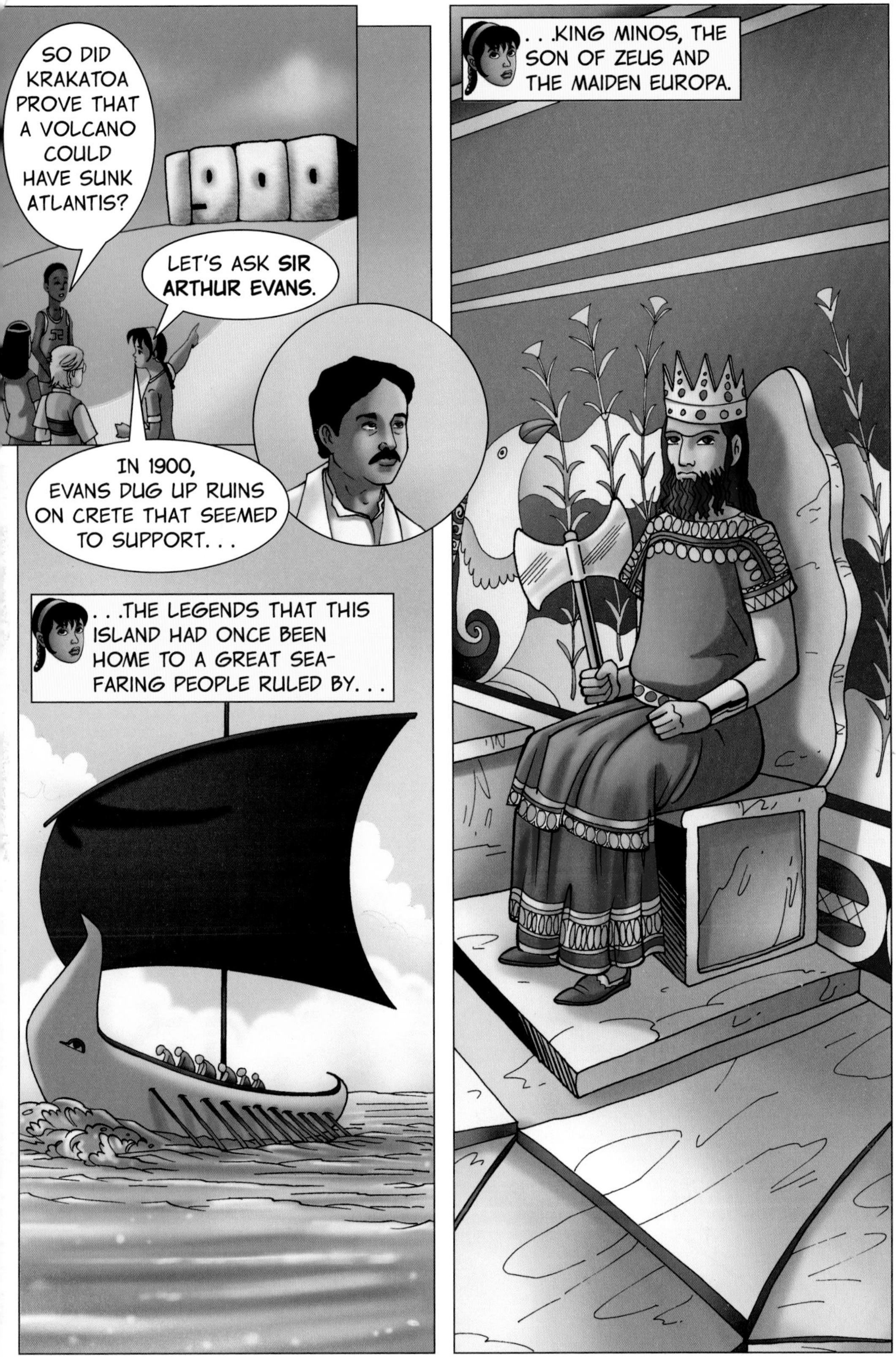

SO DID KRAKATOA PROVE THAT A VOLCANO COULD HAVE SUNK ATLANTIS?

1900

LET'S ASK SIR ARTHUR EVANS.

IN 1900, EVANS DUG UP RUINS ON CRETE THAT SEEMED TO SUPPORT. . .

. . .THE LEGENDS THAT THIS ISLAND HAD ONCE BEEN HOME TO A GREAT SEA-FARING PEOPLE RULED BY. . .

. . .KING MINOS, THE SON OF ZEUS AND THE MAIDEN EUROPA.

THE LEGEND SAYS A BRONZE ROBOT KEPT THE ISLAND SAFE FROM INTRUDERS.

KING MINOS ALSO KEPT A MONSTER IN A MAZE. LIKE THE ROBOT, THE **MINOTAUR** WAS HALF BULL AND HALF MAN!

BECAUSE HIS ARMY HAD DEFEATED THE ATHENIANS, KING MINOS DEMANDED A TRIBUTE: EVERY YEAR SEVEN YOUTHS AND SEVEN MAIDENS MUST ENTER THE MINOTAUR'S MAZE!

CHILDREN OF LOSERS MUST ENTER THE LABYRINTH!

SINCE NONE EVER CAME HOME, GREEK SHIPS RETURNING FROM MINOS'S ISLAND WOULD CHANGE THEIR SAILS FROM WHITE TO BLACK TO EXPRESS GRIEF.

WE'RE DOOMED!

IF ONLY KING MINOS WOULD HAVE MERCY!

I WONDER THE MINOTAUR IS AS HIDEOUS AS THEY SAY...

ZEUS, PLEASE SAVE US FROM YOUR SON'S MONSTER!

FREE OF THE MAZE, THE FRIENDS WERE STILL IN BIG TROUBLE!

GRUMBLE, RUMBLE, KA-BOOM!!!

IT SOUNDS LIKE KRAKATOA ONLY. . .

WHAT'S THAT NOISE?

BIGGER!

IT'S THERA!

FACT FILE

Zeus: The powerful leader of the ancient Greek gods and the protector of laws. When he became angry, Zeus threw lightning bolts! Zeus was the father of King Minos, Hercules, and many other famous mortals, as well as gods. The Romans called him Jupiter.

Olympians: The ancient Greek gods who lived on Mount Olympus, in northeastern Greece. Led by Zeus, the Olympians included 12 great gods and goddesses, as well as many other divine beings, like the **Muses**, who inspire the arts. The **Olympic Games** are named after the games originally held in honor of Zeus.

Plato: Socrates' best student. One of the super smart ancient Greeks who tried to figure out things like how the universe works and what would make a perfect society. Plato sometimes wrote down the lively dialogues that Socrates led on various subjects. The legend of Atlantis is mentioned in two of these dialogues. But Plato never finished the story, preferring to write about other things. Plato's version of the legend of Atlantis became the basis for stories, poems, paintings, songs, films, and restaurant decor.

FACT FILE

Atlas: Son of the ancient Greek god Poseidon and the mortal Cleito. When he grew up, Atlas held the sphere of the heavens on his shoulders. This can be seen in many famous paintings and statues, including one in Rockefeller Center in New York City. Because he held the world, Atlas's name became a term for a book of maps.

Crete: A mountainous island at the southern end of the Aegean Sea, now known to have been the home of the ancient Minoan civilization.

Papyrus: A water plant, *Cyperus papyrus*, with dark green stems topped with a fluffy flower. The ancient Egyptians used this reed to make boats. Since they also made writing paper from its strong stems, Egyptian paper and the books written on it are also known as papyrus.

Antideluvian: The prefix "anti" usually means "against," but in this case, it means "before the **deluge**," which is a big flood; from the Latin *diluvium*, which relates to *lavare*, meaning "to wash." Donnelly's book was about Atlantis before the disaster.